# DOLL
# TROUBLE

# HELEN V. GRIFFITH

# Doll Trouble

illustrated by
Susan Condie Lamb

GREENWILLOW BOOKS, NEW YORK

Library of Congress Cataloging-in-Publication Data

Griffith, Helen V.
    Doll trouble / by Helen V. Griffith ;
illustrated by Susan Condie Lamb.
        p.      cm.
    Summary: Caitlin's doll Holiday, who has come alive
and can walk and talk, becomes jealous when it appears
that Caitlin's old doll Jodi is also alive.
Sequel to "Caitlin's Holiday."
ISBN 0-688-12421-6
[1. Dolls—Fiction.]
I. Lamb, Susan Condie, ill.
II. Title.     PZ7.G8823Dr      1993
[Fic]—dc20      92-31510      CIP      AC

**To Carol Hurd and the
children at Hillside School,
for their good ideas**

# Contents

# Jealousy

Holiday was doing sit-ups on the bedroom windowsill while she waited for Caitlin to eat breakfast. Cars were flashing by on the street below, and once in a while someone waiting at the light would glance up and away and then back again quickly. But by the second look

9

Holiday would be perfectly still, like a normal doll. She was laughing inside, though. She knew that the person was sure he had seen her move, yet he knew that dolls couldn't move. It was Holiday's idea of a very funny joke.

Caitlin didn't like her to do it. She was afraid someone would discover that although Holiday was a twelve-inch-high doll, she could walk and talk and think just like a real person. And if that happened, Caitlin knew that scientists would take Holiday away to study her and find out how she was able to do the things she could do. Caitlin didn't want to lose Holiday. Holiday didn't want to lose Caitlin either, so she didn't play the joke very often. But now and then she just couldn't resist.

Caitlin appeared at the bedroom door.

"Let's go," she said. "I told Lauren we'd be there right after breakfast."

"Goody," Holiday said. "Don't forget my bathing suit."

Caitlin stuffed the suit into her denim bag, picked Holiday up gently by the waist, and ran down the stairs. As soon as they reached the bottom, Holiday turned into a real doll, stiff and vacant-eyed. Nobody would believe that this was the same doll that had been exercising on the windowsill a few minutes before.

Caitlin stuck her head into the kitchen. Her mother was drinking coffee and talking on the phone to one of her customers about her cosmetics order.

"Going to Lauren's," Caitlin told her.

Her mother blew her a kiss and kept on talking. Caitlin left the house and went skipping along the sidewalk.

"It's getting hot," she said, stiff-lipped. "Wish I could fit into the doll pool with you."

"And here I am in this warm-up suit," Holiday complained, also stiff-lipped.

They always talked that way outdoors because they thought it hid the fact that they were speaking together. As Caitlin had warned Holiday many times, scientists and other people interested in live dolls could be anywhere.

"Why are you worried about the warm-up suit?" Caitlin asked. "I don't think you feel hot and cold anyway."

Holiday sighed. Caitlin would never understand about fashion.

"I just like to wear the right thing," she said. "Let's stop at Rigby's Resale for a minute."

"What did I just hear!" Caitlin pretended to be aston-

**11**

ished. "The most picky, choosy, stylish doll in the world just suggested a trip to a used-clothes store. Help, I'm fainting!"

"Don't make me laugh, Caitlin," Holiday warned. "I can't laugh with stiff lips."

But she did laugh, and Caitlin did, too. They never seemed to get all the way to Lauren's without breaking the stiff-lip rule. There was always something to laugh about.

Caitlin waited at the corner for the light to change and then ran across the street to the resale shop. Inside she headed straight for the doll clothes. She knew exactly where they were because even though Holiday claimed to hate Rigby's Resale, they went there often.

With Holiday propped against a pile of picture books, Caitlin began displaying the clothes.

"Ugly," Holiday said. She said it about everything Caitlin showed her. "Ugly. Ugly. Ugly."

"I hate them all," she said finally. "Let's go."

"You're the one who wanted to come in here," Caitlin said. She held up a thin blue dress with white dots. "What about this? It looks summery."

"That's for a middle-aged doll." Holiday pouted. "Do I look middle-aged?"

# Jealousy

She fluffed out her gold-silver hair and blinked her violet eyes at Caitlin.

Caitlin giggled. "I don't think there are any middle-aged dolls."

As Holiday started to answer, she saw Mrs. Rigby approaching. At once her body became rigid, her face expressionless.

"Come on, Holiday," Caitlin said. "These clothes aren't *that* ugly."

"Are you talking to that doll?" Mrs. Rigby asked.

With a guilty start Caitlin turned around to face her.

"I never saw anybody so particular about doll dresses," Mrs. Rigby went on. "A person would almost think you were asking that doll's opinion."

Caitlin laughed in relief when she saw that Mrs. Rigby was only teasing.

"I *am* asking her opinion," she said. "And I'm sorry to say that she doesn't like anything here today."

"Well, tell her to come back tomorrow," Mrs. Rigby said, laughing heartily at the joke. "Remember, I get new old things all the time."

"I'll remember," Caitlin said.

She left the shop and lingered outside, looking at the tables piled with all kinds of useful and useless things.

"Which table did you steal me from?" Holiday asked innocently.

She liked to ask that question to see the reaction, and Caitlin didn't disappoint her.

"I didn't steal you," she said indignantly. "And you know which table it was and everything else that happened that day."

"I know, but I like to hear about it," Holiday said. "Start with how beautiful I looked."

"You were the most beautiful doll I had ever seen," Caitlin said sincerely.

"And I was lying in a box of beautiful doll clothes," Holiday prompted.

"Wonderful doll clothes," Caitlin agreed. "But it was you I wanted, not the clothes."

"So you stole me," Holiday said, with a happy wiggle.

"Stop it, Holiday," Caitlin said. "I *traded* you. I know I shouldn't have done it, but I didn't even think about it. I just took you out of the box and put my old Jodi in it."

"And you've never been sorry," Holiday said in a satisfied tone.

"Never. Except," Caitlin added, "I wish Jodi didn't belong to Jennifer now. I think Jennifer's mean to her."

14

# Jealousy

Holiday looked hard at Caitlin. Why was she worrying about Jodi? Was she beginning to regret giving her away?

"Jodi is just a doll," she said firmly. "She doesn't care about Jennifer or anything else."

Caitlin didn't answer, and Holiday felt a stab of jealousy. *She* wanted to be the one Caitlin worried about.

"Remember, Jodi has all my beautiful one-of-a-kind clothes now," she said, "while I'm wearing junk from resale shops."

"Well, at least you know where your old clothes are," Caitlin reminded her. "You get to see them often."

"And you get to see Jodi," Holiday said.

"I know. I'm glad of that." Then Caitlin sighed. "I just wish Jennifer was nicer to her."

Another jealous pang struck Holiday.

"I just wish Jennifer was nicer to the clothes," she snapped.

# CHAPTER 2

## A Pool Party

Lauren was sitting on her front step with her doll, Sandi.

"Hi, Caitlin," she said. "Sandi would say hi, too, but she has a sore throat."

"Very funny," Caitlin said, sitting beside her.

# A Pool Party

When Caitlin had first discovered what Holiday could do, she had told Lauren all about it. But Holiday wouldn't act alive in front of her, so Lauren assumed Caitlin was making believe. Now she pretended that *her* doll was alive, too.

"Sandi and I just finished jumping rope," she said. "What have you and Holiday been doing lately? Tap dancing? Horseback riding? I can just imagine Holiday sitting on a little tiny saddle on top of a big tall horse."

She was so silly that Caitlin had to laugh along with her. Holiday felt like laughing, too, but she didn't. She simply sat, looking as unaware of the world around her as Sandi did.

Caitlin held Holiday up in front of Lauren's face.

"Lauren," she said in a high-pitched voice, "you are a big dope and so is your dopey doll."

"You have a perfect doll voice," Lauren giggled.

She certainly does not, Holiday thought. I have a lovely voice.

"Come on," Lauren said. "Sandi just whispered to me that she wants to go swimming."

"Do you think she should with a sore throat?" Caitlin asked.

Lauren pretended to look into Sandi's mouth.

"All better," she reported.

The girls were on their way inside the house when they heard Jennifer calling from her doorway across the street. "Where are you going? Wait for me."

"We're taking our dolls swimming," Lauren called back.

"Wait," Jennifer yelled.

She ducked back inside the house and came out swinging her doll by the ankle and clutching doll clothes in her other hand. The doll was Caitlin's old doll, Jodi. As Caitlin stood there watching them cross the street, Holiday gave her a little pinch. It was her way of saying, "I'm your doll now. Look at me, not her." Of course, Caitlin didn't understand. She just frowned at Holiday for pinching her. But at least she stopped looking at Jodi.

The girls ran through Lauren's house and out the back door into the yard. Lauren had put the swimming pool on the grass and filled it with water from the hose.

Caitlin took off Holiday's warm-up outfit and dressed her in her new swimsuit. Holiday liked the suit because she had picked it out herself at the mall store. Most of her clothes had belonged to Jodi, and Holiday thought they were terrible.

# A Pool Party

Caitlin put sunglasses on Holiday and lowered her into the water, propping her against the side of the pool. Lauren put Sandi beside her.

"Let's see how you swim, Wendi," Jennifer said to Jodi.

Wendi was Jennifer's name for Jodi. Jennifer had no idea that Wendi/Jodi had been Caitlin's doll. All she knew was that her grandmother had given her the doll and all its beautiful clothes as a present.

Jennifer held Jodi above the pool and suddenly dropped her in. The doll hit the water with a smack that sent waves washing over her and the other dolls.

"Now you've gotten Holiday's hair all wet," Caitlin complained.

Jennifer just snickered. She kicked off her sandals and dipped her foot into the pool.

"Don't, Jennifer," Lauren told her angrily. "It's only for dolls. You'll break it."

"I just want to see if they still float after you get all the air out of them," Jennifer said.

She stepped on Jodi, pushing her to the bottom, and then with a loud screech she jerked her foot out of the pool and sat on the grass to examine it.

"Something bit me," she whimpered.

"I hope it was a spider," Caitlin said.

"A black widow," Lauren added.

"My parents will sue you if it was," Jennifer said, cheering up at the idea.

Caitlin fished Holiday out of the pool, patted her with her beach towel, and arranged her comfortably on the grass in the sun. Then she reached for Jodi, but Jennifer grabbed her first. She held her up, shook her to dry her off, and wrapped her in a piece of wrinkled cloth.

"Isn't this horrible?" Jennifer asked the other girls. "It was the only ugly thing in the box of clothes that came with my doll. I've never put it on her before, because it's so awful. But it's good enough for here."

If the girls hadn't been looking at Jodi, they would have seen Holiday's violet eyes open wide when she saw what Jodi was wearing.

My cloak! She almost cried it out loud. Jennifer has ruined it!

Jennifer dropped Jodi beside Holiday, and the girls ran off to do cartwheels across the yard. Usually Holiday liked to watch, even though she could do much better cartwheels than they could. But now she was too furious.

**20**

## A Pool Party

How could anyone say that her cloak was ugly? It was beautiful, and it had belonged to Holiday farther back than she could remember. The material was silky with metallic threads in it, silver and gold and copper. When Holiday had draped it around her shoulders and pulled the hood over her gold-silver hair, she had felt mysterious and even more beautiful than usual. And Jennifer called it ugly. Well, Jennifer was a jerk.

What a shame that such a beautiful thing was wasted on a plain, ordinary doll like Jodi. Holiday sneaked a glance at her, lying on her back in the grass where Jennifer had dropped her. She was staring straight up at the sky with sad brown eyes. Of course, they weren't really sad because Jodi didn't have any feelings.

Holiday noticed that water was dripping down the side of Jodi's face. The water almost seemed like teardrops. But of course, they weren't really teardrops. Holiday turned away, but she couldn't help looking back again. One after another the drops ran from Jodi's eyes, past her ears, and were lost in her hair.

It's pool water, Holiday told herself.

That was all it could be. After all, Jodi was just a doll. And dolls can't cry.

# DOLL TROUBLE

Unless they're like me, Holiday thought, and then she quickly reminded herself, but there aren't any other dolls like me.

She turned away from Jodi and didn't look at her anymore.

# CHAPTER 3

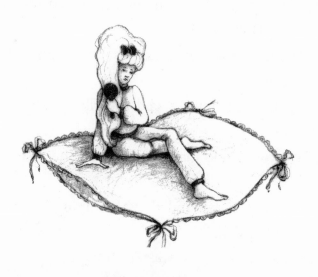

## Hurt Feelings

Caitlin didn't say a word as they walked home from Lauren's.

She's mad because of what I did to Jennifer, Holiday thought. "Well, what would *you* do if a giant foot stepped on you in a swimming pool?" she burst out resentfully.

"Huh?" Caitlin looked in surprise at the doll in her hand.

"I just don't think you should be mad at me for sticking Jennifer," Holiday said.

"I didn't know you did," Caitlin said. "I thought it was some kind of bug."

"No, it was me," Holiday said proudly. "I stuck her with my hair clip."

"Holiday, you could have really hurt her," Caitlin scolded.

"How?" Holiday demanded with an impish smile. "I'm only a little doll."

"Well," Caitlin said, "I wasn't thinking about that anyway. I was worrying about Jodi."

Worrying about Jodi! That was worse than being mad.

"I've told you a million times," Holiday said, "Jodi is just an ordinary doll. Not an intelligent and fun doll like me. Jodi is a doll doll."

"I know," Caitlin said, "but—well, it just seemed to me that Jodi looked sad today. I never thought she did before. But today she looked sad."

**24**

## Hurt Feelings

"She can't be sad. She's only a doll," Holiday insisted.

Caitlin gave Holiday a doubtful look, and then she asked, "Did that old cape she was wearing belong to you?"

Holiday nodded. "As far back as I can remember anything, I remember that cloak."

"It was beautiful, in a weird way," Caitlin said.

"Oh, I know," Holiday agreed. "I always loved it."

"And because of me, you don't have it anymore," Caitlin said regretfully.

What Holiday thought was, I'd rather have you than twenty cloaks. But Caitlin had been worrying too much about Jodi today, and Holiday didn't like it. She wanted to be the only doll on Caitlin's mind. So she looked a little sad and a little brave and said, "Oh, well."

When they got home, Caitlin said in a hesitating way, "Look, Holiday, do you mind if we don't go for our ride today? I have something else to do."

Holiday hid her disappointment. She looked forward to those afternoon bicycle basket rides. It was fun bouncing up and down with each crack in the sidewalk. But she only said, "That's fine with me. I'm a little busy myself today." Then, to prove it, she fussed with her makeup box until Caitlin left the room.

# DOLL TROUBLE

As soon as Holiday was alone, she stopped fussing and sat very still.

She doesn't want to play because she's worrying about Jodi, she thought. She's afraid Jodi is unhappy. She wishes she'd never traded us. She sighed a sad, shaky sigh. I suppose Jodi was easier to live with than I am. She never argued or begged for new clothes or played music late at night. Holiday pushed her makeup box away roughly. I bet she would if she could, though, she thought.

She grabbed her hairbrush and began to drag it through her tangled hair.

"But she can't," she told herself firmly. "She's not like me. She's an ordinary doll, and she can't do anything."

She pushed away the memory of Jodi's tears and sat on the floor for a long time, brushing and brushing her hair.

# CHAPTER 4

# The Fashion Show Contest

The next morning, when Holiday and Caitlin woke up, a steady rain was falling.

"I suppose this means no swimming," Holiday said.

"Good guess," Caitlin agreed.

The two of them were watching TV when they heard

banging at the door. Lauren and Jennifer were standing there holding big plastic bags.

"We decided this was a perfect day for a fashion show," Jennifer announced.

"*She* decided," Lauren said. "I thought it was a perfect day for staying home and eating chocolate chip cookies."

The girls peeked into the kitchen to say hello to Caitlin's mother, who was working with papers spread all over the kitchen table. Then they pounded up the stairs to Caitlin's room, sat on the floor, and dumped out the contents of their bags.

Lauren had brought Sandi and a shoe box containing Sandi's clothes.

"She doesn't have all that much," she said.

Caitlin said, "Neither does Holiday."

"Wendi does, though." Lauren pointed to Wendi, who was really Jodi. "Look at all that stuff. Jennifer, you could put on the fashion show all by yourself."

"I could, but it's more fun if we all play," Jennifer said, "so I've decided we'll have a fashion show contest."

"I never heard of a fashion show contest," Caitlin said.

# The Fashion Show Contest

"That's because I just made it up," Jennifer explained. "We each dress our doll in a certain category, and then we vote on which outfit is the prettiest."

"What if we all vote for our own dolls?" Lauren asked.

Jennifer frowned at her. "We won't if we're honest," she said.

Holiday was fuming. She knows all the clothes she has are better than anything Caitlin and Lauren have. She's just showing off. And with my clothes.

"The first category is shorts and tops," Jennifer announced.

"Tell her you won't play," Holiday whispered, but Caitlin and Lauren good-naturedly began going through their dolls' wardrobes, choosing shorts and tops for the competition.

"You go first, Lauren," Jennifer ordered.

Lauren had dressed Sandi in blue shorts and a white T-shirt. She scooted herself along on her knees as she held Sandi by the waist and trotted her across the floor to display her outfit. Caitlin and Jennifer applauded politely.

Boring, thought Holiday.

"Next," Jennifer directed.

# DOLL TROUBLE

It was Holiday's turn, and she considered *her* outfit boring, too. The green shorts and green-and-white-striped shirt had belonged to Jodi, and they weren't Holiday's taste at all.

Caitlin slid herself across the floor, skipping Holiday along beside her. Jennifer and Lauren clapped their hands.

"And now may I present the gorgeous Wendi and her wardrobe coordinator, Miss Jennifer," Jennifer announced.

The other girls laughed, but Jennifer was serious. She didn't model Wendi/Jodi on the floor. Instead she held her by one arm and skimmed her across Caitlin's bed, spinning her around and finally tossing her into the air and letting her drop with a bounce.

"Ta-da," she said. "Now let's vote. I vote for me."

"We're not voting for us," Caitlin said. "We're voting for our dolls' outfits."

"Whatever," Jennifer said. "Vote."

Of course, Wendi/Jodi's outfit won. No one would have voted against the hand-embroidered tank top and white cotton shorts that Jennifer's doll was wearing. Even though she was disgusted with the whole contest,

# The Fashion Show Contest

Holiday felt a thrill of pride. She had made the clothes herself.

If Caitlin would buy me a sewing machine, I could make more things, she thought. She had asked, but so far Caitlin hadn't bought one. Maybe she didn't believe that Holiday could really sew.

"Now," Jennifer declared, "the prom dress competition."

They all went through the motions again, Sandi in a stiff white gown with lace trim and Holiday feeling silly in a fussy orange dress that couldn't have looked good on anyone.

Did Caitlin pick this out? she wondered. We'll have to have a talk.

Jennifer spun her doll (wearing a peach silk gown designed and sewn by Holiday) across the bed, making the skirt swirl gracefully and winning three votes for Wendi/Jodi.

Next was a warm-up suit competition, then a swimsuit competition, followed by fancy jeans, rainwear, and nightgown competitions. Jennifer's doll won them all.

"And now," Jennifer announced, "the cycling outfit competition."

# DOLL TROUBLE

Caitlin and Lauren looked at each other and back at Jennifer.

"Holiday doesn't have a cycling outfit," Caitlin said.

Lauren said, "Neither does Sandi."

"I guess I win then." Jennifer smiled.

"No fair," Caitlin protested. "How can you win when there's nobody else in the contest?"

"It's still a contest whether anybody else enters or not," Jennifer said, "so I win. And now the canoeing outfit competition."

"Canoeing outfit!" Caitlin burst out laughing.

Lauren was laughing, too. "Next I suppose we'll have the mountain-climbing outfit competition," she said.

"And the whale-watching outfit competition," Caitlin added.

"And the dog-walking outfit competition," Lauren squealed.

The more Jennifer frowned, the funnier their jokes seemed to the other girls.

"We mustn't forget our bubble gum–chewing outfits," Caitlin gasped.

"And our fishbowl-cleaning outfits," Lauren choked.

Jennifer listened in disgust.

# The Fashion Show Contest

"You can laugh all you want," she said, "but I still win in every category."

Caitlin's mother came and stood in the doorway, laughing just because the girls were.

"What's going on?" she asked.

Caitlin sat up and wiped her eyes.

"Oh, Mom," she said, "I could never explain it."

"Well, after all that carrying on, you need a snack," her mother said. "I've put juice and chocolate chip cookies out on the kitchen table."

"Goody!" the girls squealed.

Caitlin and Lauren grabbed their dolls, and they all headed for the door.

"You've forgotten Wendi," Caitlin told Jennifer.

"She's not hungry," Jennifer said carelessly, leaving her lying on the floor.

Just like that, Holiday's fun was spoiled.

Caitlin's always worrying about that doll, she thought resentfully. It's not fair.

# CHAPTER 5

# A Mystery

After their snack the girls watched TV while Holiday fretted.

We could be doing something worthwhile, she thought, like shopping.

When it was time to go, Lauren ran upstairs and

came bouncing back down with Jodi and the two plastic bags of clothes. At the door Jennifer stopped and pulled her shirt collar up. "I forgot it was raining," she said. She held Jodi over her head like an umbrella and stepped outside.

Lauren jumped down the steps and stuck out her tongue to catch raindrops.

"Good-bye," they called, breaking into a splashing run.

Caitlin watched them go. "Poor Jodi," she said.

"It's only water," Holiday said.

"I know." Caitlin closed the door and carried Holiday back into the house.

They went up to the bedroom and sat side by side on the floor, folding and putting away the fashion show entries.

"Lauren and Jennifer's dolls never help them," Holiday said. "See how lucky you are to have me?"

Caitlin flashed her a smile. "I know I'm lucky to have you," she said. "Anybody can have a doll. But you're a friend, too."

Holiday's eyes shone with pleasure. "That's right. We're friends."

She picked up the green shorts she had worn for the

fashion show and was surprised to find underneath them the embroidered tank top that Jodi had modeled.

"Jennifer forgot Jodi's tank top," she said. "I don't suppose you'd let me keep it."

She glanced up at Caitlin with a mischievous smile, but Caitlin was looking into the box where she kept Holiday's clothes, and when she turned to Holiday, she wasn't smiling.

"How did these get here?" she asked.

She held up the prom dress and the fancy jeans that Jodi had worn in the fashion contest.

"I don't know," Holiday said. "How should I know?"

"Well, they didn't get there by themselves," Caitlin said, "and I didn't put them there. And Lauren and Jennifer certainly didn't put them there. And Jodi and Sandi certainly didn't put them there."

"And I certainly *certainly* didn't put them there," Holiday said indignantly.

Caitlin looked hard at Holiday. Then she threw the jeans and gown on the floor and left the room without another word. Holiday sat there stunned.

She just said we were friends, she thought, and now she thinks I stole those clothes.

## A Mystery

Holiday had never known her feelings could hurt so much.

Suddenly Caitlin came bursting back into the room. She knelt beside Holiday and touched her arm. Holiday sat very still and wouldn't look at her.

"I'm sorry I got mad like that," Caitlin said.

Holiday didn't move.

"I'm really sorry, Holiday," Caitlin repeated. "Listen. I know you want your things back, and being a doll, you probably don't understand about private property and all. Are you listening?"

Holiday still wouldn't look at Caitlin, but she did shake her head yes.

"So tomorrow I'll take the things back to Jennifer," Caitlin said, "and we'll forget all about it. Okay?"

At once Holiday's feelings stopped hurting. Caitlin really liked her. She still thought Holiday had taken the clothes, but she forgave her and liked her anyway. To Holiday that was being a real friend.

If Caitlin can forgive me for stealing the clothes, I can forgive Caitlin for thinking I did it, Holiday thought to herself. She turned and smiled up at her friend.

"Okay," Holiday said. "Let's forget it."

# CHAPTER 6

# A Spiteful Smile

Unfortunately, returning the clothes didn't go as smoothly as Caitlin and Holiday expected.

When they arrived at Lauren's, Lauren and Jennifer were just beginning a game of Monopoly on the floor of Lauren's enclosed front porch. Caitlin dropped her box of doll clothes in the corner where Sandi and Jodi were lying. Then she joined in the game, propping Holiday up nearby where she could watch.

They played for a long time, but when it looked as though Lauren might win, Jennifer began to lose interest. Instead of watching the board, she let her gaze drift around the room, and suddenly she said, "Caitlin? What is my doll's ski jacket doing in your doll's box?"

Caitlin was sitting with her back to the room, but Holiday could see her stiffen.

"I don't have your jacket," she said.

She turned around to look, and as she turned, her eyes went first to Holiday.

Not again, Holiday thought.

The lid had slid off the shoe box of Holiday's clothes, and there on top of the heap was Jodi's ski jacket. There couldn't be any doubt. There was no other ski jacket like Holiday's former ski jacket. After all, Holiday had designed it herself.

Jennifer went over and picked it up, and then her eyes got round.

"Here's Wendi's jeans," she said. "And her tank top."

Her voice got louder. "And her prom dress." She looked at Caitlin accusingly. "What else of mine have you got in here?"

She began to rummage through the box. Caitlin went over and tried to pull her away.

"That's all," she said. "You left them yesterday. I meant to tell you, but we started playing, and I forgot."

"Sure you did," Jennifer said.

"What do you think?" Caitlin demanded angrily. "That I stole them?"

"What would you think?" Jennifer asked.

Lauren broke in. "I think you forgot them and Caitlin returned them. Now come on back and finish the game."

"I didn't have the jacket with me yesterday, so I couldn't have left it," Jennifer said. "It got in that box today."

Caitlin dropped to her knees, dumped out the contents of the box, and started refilling it piece by piece, holding up each article before she dropped it in. "This is mine. This is mine. This is mine."

When she had put everything back, she picked up Holiday and the box and said, "I hope you're satisfied."

"Oh, Caitlin, don't go," Lauren begged.

# A Spiteful Smile

She jumped up to stop her and caught her foot on the edge of the Monopoly board. It upended, sending houses, hotels, and play money everywhere.

"Oh, no," Lauren wailed. "And I was winning. For the first time in my life."

She squatted on the floor and began gathering the spilled game pieces.

"Help me," she said desperately. "I remember where everything was. I had two houses on Pennsylvania Avenue and a hotel on the Boardwalk. And I was winning!"

Caitlin couldn't help laughing.

"Lauren, it's hopeless," she said, but she put down Holiday and the clothes box and helped collect the scattered bills and cards.

"The game is over, though," she said. "We could never figure out whose money was whose."

"But I was winning," Lauren moaned.

"You wouldn't have won," Jennifer said. "I would. I was just about to make a move that would have bankrupted both of you."

"Oh, Jennifer, you were not," Caitlin said.

"How do you know I wasn't?" Jennifer bristled.

"Don't start up again," Lauren pleaded. "Let's play another game."

**41**

Caitlin shook her head. "I'm not in the mood. I'm going home."

She picked up Holiday again, and as she did, Holiday could look down at the corner where Jodi and Sandi were lying. But Jodi wasn't lying down now. She was leaning against the wall facing the room. And on her face was a tiny, spiteful smile.

Jodi's gaze met Holiday's. Instantly the smile was gone, and Holiday was looking at an ordinary doll with an ordinary doll expression. But Holiday knew now that Jodi wasn't an ordinary doll. She didn't want to believe it, but she knew it was true. That mean little smile proved without a doubt that Jodi was really alive, as alive as Holiday herself.

# CHAPTER 7

# Suspicions

All the way home Holiday thought about her discovery.

I liked being the only live doll in the world, she thought with regret.

But that wasn't the worst of Jodi's being alive. Holiday's real fear was what would happen if Caitlin found out.

She worries enough about her now when she thinks she's just a plain doll, Holiday thought anxiously. What will she do if she finds out that Jodi has feelings?

But maybe she would never find out. Jodi seemed to want to keep the fact that she was alive a secret from everyone, both humans and dolls.

I wonder why, Holiday mused, and then with a little shock she thought, Jodi is the one who is moving the clothes around!

But why would she bother doing such a silly thing? Then Holiday remembered Jodi's small, secret smile.

She hopes Caitlin will blame me, she thought. She wants to cause trouble between me and Caitlin.

Holiday was so furious that she could hardly keep from telling Caitlin what she had just figured out. But what would Caitlin do if she knew? Would she worry about Jodi even more than she did now? Would she try to get her back? Holiday decided she didn't dare tell Caitlin that her old doll was alive. But she was afraid of what Jodi might do next.

She hates me because I'm Caitlin's doll now, Holiday

# Suspicions

thought. Jodi hates me, and she's going to try to make Caitlin hate me, too.

She was so busy with her own thoughts that she didn't know Caitlin was angry until they were home. As soon as they got upstairs, Caitlin dumped Holiday on the bed and said furiously, "You did it again."

"What did I do?" Holiday asked. "I didn't do anything."

"You know what you did," Caitlin said. "That jacket."

"I never touched that jacket," Holiday denied energetically, but Caitlin cut her off.

"Why are you doing it?" she asked. "You know I wouldn't let you keep stolen things. All you're doing is making me look bad. Is that what you want?"

"I didn't do anything," Holiday insisted.

"Jennifer blames me," Caitlin went on. "Even Lauren is beginning to wonder."

"Then she's no friend," Holiday said. "A friend wouldn't suspect another friend of something if the friend told her friend that she didn't do it. Isn't that right?"

"What?" Caitlin asked, looking confused.

"I didn't do it," Holiday said.

"I want to believe you, Holiday," Caitlin told her.

"Then believe me," Holiday said.

There was a long pause, and then Caitlin said, "I'll try." She walked to the door. "I have to go out now. I'll see you later."

"Okay," Holiday said.

Neither of them smiled.

# CHAPTER 8

# Jennifer's Big News

The next day Caitlin and Lauren were sitting on Lauren's steps asking each other riddles when Jennifer called from across the street.

"Come on over," she yelled. "I have big news!"

Holiday nearly fainted.

She's found out about Jodi, she thought. She knows Jodi's alive.

"We're comfortable," Lauren yelled back. "You come over here."

"I have to stay with my brothers," Jennifer shouted. "Come on."

Caitlin and Lauren looked at each other and sighed.

"Those brothers," Caitlin said.

"They're everywhere at once, like two squirrels," Lauren said.

"Like two *noisy* squirrels," Caitlin said.

The girls picked up their dolls and crossed over to Jennifer's side of the street.

"What's the big news?" Lauren asked.

"Come in and I'll tell you," Jennifer said, looking mysterious and important.

They followed Jennifer into the house. It was built just like Caitlin's and Lauren's and all the other rows of houses in the neighborhood. There was a front porch that led into a living room where the stairway to the bedrooms was located. Behind the living room was a dining room; behind that were the kitchen and back steps leading to a small backyard.

# Jennifer's Big News

Jennifer led them into the living room.

"Sit down," she said in a low voice. "I don't want my brothers to hear."

Holiday could hardly bear the suspense. If Jennifer had discovered that Jodi was alive, why didn't she just say it? She certainly didn't have to worry about her brothers hearing. They were making so much noise upstairs that they wouldn't have heard if she had screamed the news at the top of her lungs.

Caitlin looked toward the ceiling.

"What are they doing up there?" she asked.

"Playing," Jennifer said unconcernedly.

Holiday was wondering where Jodi was. If she were really alive, wouldn't Jennifer want to show her off? But maybe she was alive only for Jennifer the way that Holiday was alive only for Caitlin. No, in that case there wouldn't be any use in telling anyone at all. No one would believe it, and there was no way to prove it.

"Jennifer," Lauren said impatiently, "do you have any news or not?"

Jennifer gave an excited bounce. "I do," she said. "Guess what!"

"Oh, Jennifer," Caitlin said, "how can we guess? It could be anything."

"Okay, I'll give you a hint," Jennifer said.

Just then a cat streaked down the stairs and dived under the sofa. Immediately Jennifer's brothers came tumbling after the cat.

"Where's Zorro?" they yelled.

"I don't think he feels like playing," Jennifer said with a laugh.

"We have to question him," Skip explained. "He's from an evil planet."

"He's only a cat," Caitlin said.

"He's in disguise," Matt told her confidentially.

They looked under all the furniture, pulling out a variety of books and toys, until they found the cat. Zorro, looking resigned, was carried back upstairs.

"Poor Zorro," Caitlin said.

"Don't feel sorry for Zorro," Jennifer said. "He's as bad as the boys. He bats my dolls around and makes beds out of their clothes."

Holiday nearly shuddered. A cat sleeping on her beautiful things! But it was nice to know he was rough on Jennifer's dolls, since that must include Jodi.

The boys' search had solved the mystery of Jodi's

whereabouts. She was one of the objects pulled out from under the sofa, still wrapped in Holiday's beautiful old cloak.

"So that's where she got to," Jennifer said, but she left her lying there.

The boys hadn't been back upstairs a minute when there was a piercing shriek. The three girls exchanged startled looks, and all ran upstairs together. The cat came slinking down the stairs past them and disappeared under the sofa.

Holiday slid off her chair and knelt beside Jodi.

"Hi there, Jodi," she said.

There was no reaction from the doll.

"Or do you prefer Wendi?" Holiday asked. "Hi there, Wendi."

There was no answer. Holiday shook Jodi's shoulder.

"I know you're alive," she said.

A low growl came from under the sofa, and Holiday looked around to see Zorro watching her with surprised but interested eyes. His tail was switching back and forth like a whip.

"Don't get any ideas," Holiday warned him. "I'm no mouse."

At that moment she realized that the excitement was

over upstairs and the girls were coming down. It was too late to climb back onto her chair, so Holiday dropped to the floor, lying rigidly beside Jodi. Zorro came out from under the sofa and sniffed at her curiously.

"Bad cat," Jennifer scolded. "Scratching a little boy and then going after Caitlin's doll."

She stamped her foot, and Zorro ran. Holiday felt a little guilty for getting him into more trouble, but not too guilty. He probably got away with plenty.

Caitlin picked Holiday up, straightened her clothes, and put her back on the chair. Then she lifted Jodi out of the heap of toys, smoothed the stiff, metallic fabric of the old cloak, and ran her hand over the doll's messy auburn hair. Gently she placed Jodi on the chair with Holiday.

She never looks at me like that, Holiday thought jealously, resisting an urge to punch Jodi.

"Now maybe I can tell you my news," Jennifer said. She cocked an ear toward the stairs. The boys were playing noisily again. "I'm not supposed to tell them yet because as soon as they know, they won't want to wait."

# Jennifer's Big News

"Wait for what?" Lauren asked. "You haven't told us anything yet."

"We're moving," Jennifer said excitedly. "We're selling this house and moving away."

Holiday's first happy thought was, She doesn't know Jodi's alive. Her second was, She'll take Jodi away with her. Good!

"Why are you moving?" Caitlin asked. "Is your father being transferred?"

"No," Jennifer said. "We're moving to a better neighborhood."

"A better neighborhood!" Lauren echoed. "Where could you find a better neighborhood?"

"There are lots of better neighborhoods," Jennifer told her.

"Neighborhoods with a sub shop right down the street?" Lauren asked.

"And a resale shop a block away?" Caitlin asked.

"Your new house must be next door to Disney World," Lauren said.

"It must be *in* Disney World," Caitlin said.

"It's not in Disney World." Jennifer was starting to get mad, but then she saw that the girls were joking.

"You can come and see me when I move," she told them.

"Do you think we'd better?" Caitlin asked. "What if we like the neighborhood so much we won't leave?"

"I'm not worried," Jennifer said. "No matter how nice the neighborhood is, Matt and Skip will be there. The houses on either side of us will be up for sale within a week."

# CHAPTER 9

# A Surprise for Caitlin

The girls never got around to playing. Jennifer was full of talk about the new house, and every now and then they all had to run upstairs and investigate a thud or a scream or a crash.

# DOLL TROUBLE

Holiday was bored. After a while she drifted off to sleep, and she didn't wake up until Caitlin was leaving.

"Come over tomorrow," Jennifer was saying. "I have to stay with the brats again."

Caitlin swung her denim bag over her shoulder and reached for Holiday.

"There's something hanging out of your bag," Lauren said.

Caitlin looked down. "What is this?" she asked, pulling on a piece of stiff, glittery fabric.

The sight of the cloth brought Holiday wide awake. She recognized it right away. It was her old cloak, the one Jodi had been wearing. Somehow she had managed to stuff it into Caitlin's bag.

She's trying to make trouble for me again, Holiday thought.

Then she realized something else: When she had gone to sleep, Jodi was sitting beside her. But Jodi wasn't there now. Holiday braced herself. She knew something bad was about to happen.

Caitlin opened her bag and looked inside. Her expression told Holiday that her fears were right. Caitlin reached into her bag and pulled out the old cloak—and Jodi, too.

## A Surprise for Caitlin

I should never have gone to sleep, Holiday thought with a sinking feeling. I should have watched her.

There was an ominous silence in the room. Then Jennifer demanded, "How did Wendi get into your bag?"

Caitlin couldn't seem to believe what she was seeing. In slow motion she looked from Jodi to Jennifer and back again.

"I have to go," she muttered, thrusting Wendi/Jodi into Jennifer's hands.

She grabbed Holiday and almost ran out the door, jumping recklessly down the front steps in one leap.

"Holiday," she whispered wrathfully, "I'm never going to speak to you again."

She practically ran down the street, jerking Holiday along by one arm.

"Slow down," Holiday gasped, but Caitlin just moved faster.

"Stealing a whole doll," she panted, "just to get her clothes."

Holiday knew it was the wrong time to laugh, but she couldn't help it. "If you think I stole Jodi, you must think I'm a weight lifter," she said with a giggle.

"You don't care how you make me look to my friends.

You don't care how I feel." Angry as she was, Caitlin was still trying to talk stiff-lipped. But her lips were quivering as she said, "All you ever think about are your precious clothes."

Holiday stopped laughing. This was serious. Caitlin was mad. She was thinking mean things about Holiday. But even worse, Caitlin was sad. Holiday couldn't stand to see her sad. She hated to do it, but she saw that she would have to tell Caitlin about Jodi. Otherwise she would keep blaming Holiday for Jodi's dirty tricks, and they would never have fun anymore.

"Can we go somewhere private?" Holiday asked. "I have something important to say."

"Say it then," Caitlin's tone was not encouraging.

"It's too important to say in the middle of the sidewalk," Holiday said.

Caitlin frowned, but she walked to the public telephone on the corner and put Holiday on the shelf. She stood so that her body hid the doll from passersby. Then she picked up the receiver and spoke into it.

"All right. What's so important?" she demanded.

"Why are you talking into the phone?" Holiday asked.

# A Surprise for Caitlin

"So I can move my lips," Caitlin snapped. "What's so important?"

It was hard to begin. Finally Holiday said, "You should never have thought that I put Jodi in your bag because I didn't. But I know how she got there."

Holiday waited for some reaction, but Caitlin didn't say anything at all.

"Don't you want to know how she got there?" Holiday asked.

Caitlin spoke into the telephone, but she was looking in a very unpleasant way at Holiday.

"Let me guess," she said. "The cat did it. A hurricane blew her in. She crawled in by herself."

"That's right!" Holiday said excitedly. "You're right!"

"What's right?" Caitlin asked. "The cat? The hurricane?"

"No, not the cat and the hurricane," Holiday said. "Your third guess. Jodi crawled in there by herself."

Caitlin hung up the phone disgustedly.

"Holiday," she said, "I'm not nearly as dumb as you seem to think."

"I know it's hard to believe since she wasn't alive when you had her," Holiday said. "But all the evidence points to it. Listen—"

"No," Caitlin interrupted. "All the evidence points to you."

There was a long, cold silence while Holiday and Caitlin stared into each other's eyes. Then Holiday said evenly, "When we left Jennifer's, you said you were never going to speak to me again. When does that start?"

"Right now," Caitlin said.

"That's good," Holiday said, "because I'm never going to speak to you again, either."

And all the way home neither one said a word.

## ◇ C H A P T E R  1 0 ◇

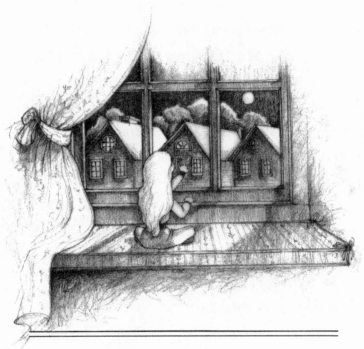

# A Serious Fight

When they got home, Caitlin ran directly to her room. She threw her bag on the bed, set Holiday down on the floor, and without a word left the room. Tight-lipped, Holiday watched her go.

I'm really never going to speak to her again, she

thought. Never. Ever. She thought with satisfaction of how sorry Caitlin would be when she realized that Holiday really meant it. She'll get tired of not talking and she'll say things to me, but I won't answer, Holiday thought. And when she finds out how wrong she was about me, she'll be so sorry. But it will be too late.

Holiday sat on the floor hugging her knees, trying to be glad about how sorry Caitlin would be.

But if I don't talk, I'll be just like any other doll, she fretted. What good is that?

She got to her feet and began to roam aimlessly around the room. She didn't know what to do with herself. Usually she liked to try new eye makeup combinations or dance to the stereo or invent hairstyles. But today nothing seemed fun.

"Being mad is boring," she said out loud.

She climbed up the curtain to the windowsill and then sat there in the bright sunshine, staring dully out at the street. The front door slammed, and Caitlin came into view, walking hurriedly along the sidewalk.

She's going out to play without me, Holiday thought, and she surprised herself by starting to cry.

She brushed away her tears angrily and looked for Caitlin again, but she was out of sight. For a long time

## A Serious Fight

Holiday sat on the sill, watching without interest as neighbors walked up and down the sidewalk, as customers entered and left the sub shop across the street, as cars stopped at the traffic light and then drove on. With a faint feeling of surprise she saw Caitlin come out of the resale shop up the street.

We always went there together, Holiday thought, and she had to fight off another rush of tears.

The door slammed as Caitlin came into the house, and Holiday tensed. How would they act when they were face-to-face again? Angry? Friendly? Sorry? She couldn't decide, but it didn't matter. Caitlin didn't come upstairs.

Holiday sat on the windowsill, feeling worse and worse every minute. She saw Caitlin's father come home from work. Usually she and Caitlin sat out on the steps waiting for him. They would compete to see who was first to catch sight of his green pickup truck coming up the street. Caitlin was down there now. Holiday couldn't see the steps from where she sat, but she heard Caitlin's greeting and her father's answer as they went inside the house together.

Holiday sat leaning against the window frame as the hours went by. The sky behind the rooftops changed from brilliant blue to pinkish to gray. Lights began to show from the windows of the houses throughout the neighborhood. Cars turned on their headlights. The sky turned black.

When the lights went out in the sub shop, Holiday came to with a jolt.

It's late, she thought. I've been sitting here for hours. Just sitting. Not even thinking.

Terror swept over her, and she jumped to her feet. I'm turning into an ordinary doll. Sitting around being sad is turning me into an ordinary doll.

Holiday had never been so scared in her life.

"It's not going to happen," she promised herself. "I won't let it."

The bedroom light flashed on, and Caitlin came in. Holiday forgot all about not speaking. The only thing in her mind was her fear of becoming an ordinary doll.

"I can't stay here," she blurted out.

Caitlin stared at her.

"I'm too sad," Holiday said, and when Caitlin didn't speak, she said, "I have to go away."

"You want to go to Jennifer's, don't you?" Caitlin said coldly.

# A Serious Fight

Holiday was shocked. That wasn't what she wanted at all. How could Caitlin even think it?

"You don't understand," she said.

"Yes, I do," Caitlin said. "You want to go live with your stupid clothes."

At those words Holiday saw red.

"And you want your stupid Jodi," she stormed. "So you might as well just trade us back again and then everybody will be happy."

Holiday clambered down from the windowsill and stalked across the floor without looking at Caitlin. It would have been nice to walk right out of the room, but there was nowhere she could go, so she flung herself onto her bed with her face to the wall.

All the time that Caitlin was getting undressed and into bed, Holiday never moved, but inside her head her thoughts were running around and around.

She and Jodi can have each other, she thought bitterly, and I'll go far away. And someday Caitlin will be sorry she was so mean, and she'll look for me everywhere. But I'll be gone without a trace.

Holiday found herself smiling. It was very interesting to think of Caitlin traveling the world looking for her lost Holiday.

# DOLL TROUBLE

Sometimes she'll almost catch up with me, Holiday imagined, but I'll have just left like an hour before. She'll be really sad because by then she'll know that Jodi is a troublemaker and no fun and I was perfect.

A problem occurred to Holiday. Caitlin wouldn't realize that Holiday was perfect because she would still think she was the one who had taken the clothes. Jodi certainly wasn't going to admit it if she didn't have to.

Before I go without a trace, Holiday decided, Caitlin has to know the facts about those clothes.

That meant making Jodi talk to Caitlin. Holiday had no doubt that she would be able to find a way to do that. Of course, when Jodi confessed, Caitlin would be sorry she had been so unfair. She would beg Holiday's forgiveness. But it would be too late. With a dignified farewell Holiday would walk proudly and bravely out of Caitlin's life forever.

Just like a movie, Holiday thought, wriggling with excitement.

She couldn't wait to get started on Jodi. She went to sleep planning what she would wear for the good-bye scene.

# CHAPTER 11

## Holiday Throws Things

Holiday woke up refreshed and cheerful and ready for action. It was time to start on her project of getting Jodi to talk, first to her and then to Caitlin. She wasn't sure how long it would take, and she didn't have forever. It had to happen before Jennifer's family moved away.

**67**

She was dressed and had tried her hair six different ways before Caitlin got up.

"Good morning," Holiday sang out. "It's a beautiful day for visiting."

Caitlin, looking mussed and glum, eyed her suspiciously. Holiday remembered then that they had gone to bed mad at each other. She'd been having so much fun making plans that she had forgotten why she was doing it.

Caitlin left the room, and Holiday heard the shower begin running. It would be awhile before Caitlin was ready to leave for Jennifer's. Holiday was too excited to sit still. She climbed up on the windowsill and startled motorists. Then she played trampoline on the bed until Caitlin, less mussed but still glum, came back into the room to dress.

"Turn on your radio for me," Holiday said. "I'll listen to music while you're having breakfast."

Caitlin gave her a grumpy look, but she turned on the radio before she left the room. Holiday slid off the bed and began to dance to the music.

Jodi might be able to walk, she thought, but I'll bet she can't dance like this.

When the song ended, a voice began reporting news.

## Holiday Throws Things

Holiday found that it wasn't fun to dance to news reports. She began to wonder why Caitlin didn't come back. She went to the bedroom door and looked out into the hall. Nobody was around, but she could hear voices coming from downstairs. She went to the head of the stairs and listened. The talking was coming from the TV, she decided, but from her position she couldn't see into the living room. Holiday slid down a few steps, and then she saw Caitlin, lying on her stomach in front of the set, her hands under her chin and her feet in the air. She didn't look as if she planned to go anywhere.

Holiday bit her lip in frustration. She and Caitlin went to Lauren's or Jennifer's to play nearly every morning. Now, just when it was important for Holiday to see Jodi, Caitlin had a sudden interest in TV.

Holiday leaned out between the banister posts. Caitlin's mother didn't seem to be around. She was probably on the phone in the kitchen or in the backyard working in her garden.

"Caitlin!" Holiday whispered.

Caitlin didn't turn around. Holiday called a little louder, but the TV noise kept Caitlin from hearing. Holiday hoped it would keep Caitlin's mother from hearing, too.

# DOLL TROUBLE

Holiday kept calling, a little louder each time, and finally she yelled at the top of her voice, "Caitlin!" but it was no use. Her doll voice wasn't strong enough.

She would have to attract Caitlin's attention some other way. Maybe if she threw something. Holiday climbed up the stairs and ran back into the bedroom. What could she use? A shoe, she decided. She would throw a shoe, hit Caitlin, and Caitlin would look up and see her. And it wouldn't hurt her. Holiday's shoes were little.

She grabbed the heaviest pair she had. They weren't really very heavy, but maybe they would do the job. She returned to her position on the stair, leaned out, and attempted an underhand pitch toward Caitlin. The shoe flipped straight up and then landed on the floor just below Holiday.

"Oops," she said.

She aimed the second shoe more carefully. It landed with a soundless plop about a yard from Caitlin's elbow.

Holiday hurried back upstairs for more ammunition. She pulled the pillowcase off her pillow and stuffed it with shoes, and then looked around for other things to put in it. Her tennis racket, that would be good to throw, and her sunglasses, and her pocketbook. With an effort she dragged the loaded pillowcase back to her perch on the stairway and dumped everything out on the step. Then she started throwing things.

The first two shoes bounced uselessly across the floor.

"I can do better than that," Holiday encouraged herself.

She took careful aim with the next shoe. It flew through the air and landed on Caitlin's back.

"Yay!" Holiday yelled, but Caitlin just reached around and scratched the place where she had been hit. When she moved, the shoe fell unnoticed to the floor.

They're too light, Holiday decided, but one by one she threw the rest of them anyway because she liked watching them bounce. By the time Holiday was finished, there were little shoes on the rug and on the chairs and a tiny red sandal had ended up in a candy dish.

It'll be fun if somebody tries to eat it, Holiday thought.

When the shoes were gone, Holiday tried to throw

the pillowcase, but it just floated down and draped itself over a lampshade. Caitlin was still engrossed in the TV, laughing now and then, but mostly just staring.

This is so ridiculous. Holiday fretted. Why can't she turn around just once?

She had two more things to throw. She tried the sunglasses first, although she didn't expect them to do any good and they didn't. They went much farther than she intended and snagged on a picture frame, where they hung like a tiny ornament.

"Pretty," Holiday said.

That left the tennis racket. Holiday had high hopes for the tennis racket. It was heavier than the other things she had thrown.

All I have to do is take my time, she thought, and aim slowly and carefully, and bounce this racket right off her head. That will make her look.

It was hard to get into a good throwing position because of the banister posts. Holiday leaned out between them, and then she leaned a little farther, and then she leaned out a little too far. When she threw the tennis racket, somehow she threw herself, too.

She thumped down on the rug at about the same time that the tennis racket bounced off Caitlin's head, and only seconds before Caitlin's mother walked into the room.

"I wish you wouldn't leave your toys lying around," she told her daughter. "Somebody could trip."

Caitlin rubbed the back of her head and looked around with a puzzled expression on her face. And Holiday came very close to giggling out loud.

# CHAPTER 12

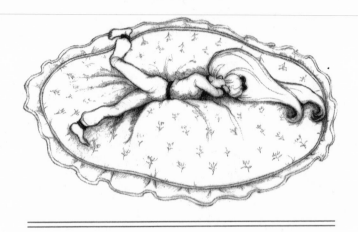

# Holiday Throws a Tantrum

"Holiday," Caitlin said when they were back in the bed-room, "sometimes you don't make sense."

She had gathered up all the shoes (Holiday was sorry nobody would try to eat the one in the candy dish), collected the pillowcase, the sunglasses, and the tennis racket, and carried them and Holiday upstairs.

"I had to talk to you," Holiday said.

"I see," Caitlin said. "So of course, you had to throw your shoes all over the room."

"I yelled first," Holiday explained. "You couldn't hear me."

"If it was so important, why didn't you just come downstairs?" Caitlin asked.

"I was afraid your mother would see me," Holiday said impatiently. She didn't want to talk. She wanted to go to Jennifer's.

"If my mother came in, you could have just acted like a doll," Caitlin said. "You've done it before."

"Well, I didn't think of it, okay?" Holiday said. "I have other things on my mind right now."

Caitlin snorted. "What could a doll have to think about?"

Holiday could have reeled off a whole list of things, but enough time had been wasted this morning. "When are we going to Jennifer's?" she asked.

"Jennifer's!" Caitlin gave Holiday a grim look. "After what you did yesterday, she probably wouldn't let me in the door."

"I didn't do it," Holiday said. "And yes, she would."

"Well, I wouldn't go, anyway," Caitlin said. "I wouldn't feel right. Even Lauren looked at me funny when I pulled Jodi out of my bag."

"I want to go to Jennifer's," Holiday said.

Caitlin was busy putting away the shoes and inserting Holiday's pillow back into the pillowcase.

"Caitlin," Holiday said, "I want to go to Jennifer's."

Caitlin shrugged. "Then go."

"Don't be funny," Holiday said. "It's important."

Caitlin put down the pillow and looked at Holiday.

"Why is it important for you to go to Jennifer's?" she asked. "Did you think of something else she has that you want?"

Holiday decided not to get mad at Caitlin's remark. It was more important right now to think up a reason why she had to go to Jennifer's. Should she tell the truth? That she was going to make Jodi admit that she was the clothes stealer? No, there was no use in that. Caitlin was sure Jodi wasn't alive, just because she had never seen her do anything.

Holiday would have to invent a reason then. She didn't like to do it, and she wasn't very good at it, either, but this was an emergency.

## Holiday Throws a Tantrum

"I lost a—uh—a valuable necklace," she blurted out.

Caitlin laughed. "Holiday, you don't have a valuable necklace."

"Well, not worth a lot of money," Holiday explained quickly. "But this necklace had great sentimental value."

Even to Holiday it sounded made up.

"How could you have a necklace with great sentimental value?" Caitlin asked. "All your jewelry was Jodi's until recently."

"That's it," Holiday exclaimed. "I have to find the necklace because it was Jodi's, and someday she might want it back."

Caitlin shook her head. "Jodi is a doll. Nothing matters to her."

Holiday could see that the necklace story was a failure. She would have to think of something else quickly. She had to get to Jodi as soon as possible. For all she knew, Jennifer's family might be going to move tomorrow. Then she might never have a chance to talk to Jodi again.

Suddenly Holiday did what she always did when nothing else worked. She threw herself on the floor. She banged her fists. She kicked her feet. She had a tantrum.

"I want to go to Jennifer's!" she yelled. "I want to go to Jennifer's!"

Finally she got tired of yelling. She raised her head and looked for Caitlin. Caitlin was sitting on her bed, holding her denim bag and Holiday's box of clothes.

"When you're finished," she said, "we can go."

# CHAPTER 13

# In the Medicine Cabinet

Jennifer and Lauren were sitting on Jennifer's steps. They looked a little bored. Maybe that was why they greeted Caitlin in such a friendly way.

"Hi, Caitlin," Lauren called. "We were just wondering what to do."

"I told you we could have a fashion contest," Jennifer said.

Caitlin and Lauren looked at each other and grinned.

"One was enough," Lauren said.

"Well, let's go in," Jennifer said. "It's getting hot out here."

When they walked through the front porch into the living room, the three girls stopped in surprise. The furniture cushions had been propped against the sofa and chairs to form tunnels, and they could hear Jennifer's brothers making train noises under the cushions.

"So that's why they were so quiet," Jennifer said.

Matt, going "Whooo, whooo," came crawling out of the tunnel. When he saw the girls, he yelled, "Yipe!," jumped to his feet, and pelted upstairs, his brother right behind him.

"They know I'll make them stop and straighten this up." Jennifer laughed. "They're not allowed to play with the cushions."

"It looks like fun," Lauren said. She crawled inside. "It's like a little house." She propped Sandi against the wall. "And you're the little owner," she said. "And here comes a little visitor."

# In the Medicine Cabinet

Caitlin crawled in the other end and propped Holiday beside Sandi.

"Here comes another visitor," Jennifer said, and she crawled in and tossed Jodi over by the other dolls. "Isn't this snug? I haven't done this in years."

"I've never played in cushions before," Lauren said.

"You've never made forts and tunnels and play-houses?" Jennifer asked.

"I never even thought of it," Lauren admitted.

"Well, if my mom catches us, we're in trouble," Jennifer warned. "She says it dirties the cushions."

Suddenly there were cries of "Earthquake! Earthquake!" and the top of the tunnel caved in.

"Ow!" Jennifer yelled. "That hurt!"

The girls looked out over the fallen cushions at the boys, who were jumping up and down and shouting with laughter.

"You brats!" Caitlin shouted.

"It was an earthquake," Matt screamed.

"We're lucky the house is still standing," Skip screeched.

"In a minute you'll wish the house fell on you," Jennifer said in a threatening voice.

With happy shrieks the boys turned and ran, the three girls right behind them.

Holiday heard the screened door bang and knew they had run outside. She waited, listening, but they didn't come back in. She could hear laughter coming from the yard. It didn't sound as if anything too terrible were happening to the boys. Too bad. But their prank had given her a chance for some conversation with Jodi. Holiday had been thrown clear when the cushions collapsed, but Jodi was underneath somewhere.

"Jodi, where are you?" Holiday whispered.

There was no answer. Holiday hadn't really expected any. She finally found Jodi wedged between a cushion and the sofa, lying on her back on the floor.

"Jodi," Holiday said, "we have to talk."

Jodi's expression didn't change.

"Jodi," Holiday said, "stop wasting time. Talk to me."

Jodi still didn't answer, and Holiday felt herself getting angry.

"You'd better talk to me," she began again, but just then the boys reappeared, breathless and giggling. Instantly Holiday dropped to the floor and lay there stiff and still.

"There's one," Skip whispered loudly.

# In the Medicine Cabinet

He grabbed Holiday and then saw Jodi lying under the cushion.

"Here's another one," he chortled. "There's one more somewhere."

The boys threw cushions aside until they found Sandi, and then they stood with their ears cocked toward the back door.

"They're still doing cartwheels," Matt said.

"Let's hurry, anyway," Skip urged. "Where shall we hide them?"

They looked quickly around the room.

"Not here," Skip decided. "Let's go upstairs."

They ran up the steps, laughing with excitement. Holiday was irked. What were these little pests up to? They had run into Jennifer's bedroom.

"Not here," Skip said. "She'll find them right away in here."

"I know where," Matt yipped, and he dashed from the bedroom into the bathroom.

Now what? Holiday wondered as she and the other dolls were whisked across the hallway.

Matt opened the medicine cabinet over the washbowl and surveyed the filled shelves.

"They'll never fit in there," Skip said.

"I'll make them fit," Matt told him.

He emptied the top shelf and put the things on the other shelves. Then he put Jodi in the space he had made.

"See?" he said.

"But what about the other two?" Skip asked. "You'll have to empty the cabinet."

"If I did that, Jennifer would know right away where the dolls were," Matt objected.

He picked Holiday up and tried to place her in various locations in the medicine cabinet. Finally he shoved her onto the bottom shelf on top of a row of bottles and jars.

"Listen!" Skip hissed.

The boys stood still, quivering like hunted rabbits.

"They're coming!" Matt squealed.

He slammed the door shut on Holiday, and she heard them run out of the bathroom and thud down the stairs.

"I can't believe this," Holiday said. "How long do they expect me to stay in here?"

She tried to straighten up, and her arm went up to the elbow into a jar of gooey cream.

"How disgusting," she said.

## In the Medicine Cabinet

Holiday could hear loud voices coming from down-stairs, but she couldn't make out the words. Then the voices came nearer, along with the pounding of many feet on the stairs.

"You're hurting my arm," Matt wailed.

Good, Holiday thought.

"Whatever it is, we didn't do it," Skip was insisting.

Ha, thought Holiday.

"We saw you coming down the stairs," Jennifer said. "Those dolls are up here someplace."

"Dolls? What dolls?" Matt asked in an overly innocent tone.

"Yeah, what dolls?" Skip tried to sound innocent, too, but he was laughing too hard to be convincing.

There was a shout from Jennifer. "Here's Lauren's doll in my bedroom. The other two must be here someplace."

Holiday heard the other girls rush to Jennifer's bedroom while the boys stood in the hall and giggled.

They must have thrown her there before they went downstairs, she thought. Those brats.

Holiday could hear thumps and bumps coming from Jennifer's bedroom. It sounded as though the girls were tearing the room apart, looking for her and Jodi.

# DOLL TROUBLE

They'll never look in here, she thought. I'm going to have to spend the day in a medicine cabinet.

"Any luck yet?" she heard Skip call to the girls.

"Have you checked with Zorro?" Matt asked, and both boys snorted with laughter.

Then Holiday heard them run screaming down the stairs. The girls must have come out of the bedroom.

"Oh, let them go," she heard Jennifer say. "When my parents get home, they'll make them tell."

The girls' voices faded as they went downstairs, and Holiday settled herself as comfortably as she could among the bottles, tubes, and jars to wait. Being a doll, she was used to waiting, but usually she had a more pleasant place to pass the time than a bathroom medicine cabinet. There was one good thing about it, though. It was a perfect place for a private talk. Holiday looked at Jodi lying on the glass shelf above her.

"Jodi," she said firmly, "I know you're alive, and I know what you're trying to do to me. There's no use pretending anymore. You have to talk to me."

She waited, giving Jodi plenty of time to decide to answer, but there was no answer.

"Why are you doing it, Jodi?" Holiday persisted. "You

# In the Medicine Cabinet

have to tell me, and you have to tell Caitlin. Do you understand?"

There was no sound from the shelf above. Jodi was lying on her back, so Holiday couldn't see her face. There was no way to know if her words were making any impression. A feeling of discouragement crept over Holiday. She had been so sure that she could make Jodi speak to her. Now it seemed that she had been wrong. Suddenly her eyes burned, and she knew that she was going to cry.

"Jodi, it's important," she said. "You have to tell Caitlin that I'm not taking the clothes. That's all you have to do, and then I'm going away forever, because you're the one she wants, not me. But you have to tell her."

Holiday couldn't say any more. She was crying too hard. And still, Jodi never said a word.

It's no use, Holiday thought hopelessly. She's not going to answer me.

She almost wondered if she was mistaken and Jodi really was only a doll. She stopped crying and went back to just waiting. A lot of time seemed to go by. After a while she knew that Caitlin must have gone home without her. She wondered if leaving her had made Caitlin sad. Or was she more worried about what had happened to Jodi?

Now and then she could hear someone enter the bathroom, but no one opened the medicine cabinet.

Somebody is going to get a surprise, she thought, and in spite of everything, the corners of her mouth twitched. She began to look forward to the opening of the cabinet door.

# CHAPTER 14

## Conversation on a Bear

Holiday was passing the time thinking up a dream wardrobe when the medicine cabinet door suddenly opened. With nothing to brace herself against, she landed with a clatter in the washbowl. Jennifer was staring at her openmouthed, while the boys whooped with laughter in the doorway. Jennifer began to laugh, too.

"So this is why you wouldn't go to bed until I did," she said.

"We wanted to see you find them," Skip told her, grinning from ear to ear.

"You were surprised, weren't you?" Matt giggled.

"I was. I'd forgotten all about those dolls. You little brats," Jennifer added affectionately.

Holiday was disappointed. She had hoped for a bigger reaction than that. Jennifer wasn't even mad.

Still chuckling, Jennifer plucked Jodi off the top shelf of the cabinet. She threw the two dolls into a corner of her bedroom already cluttered with assorted toys and games. Then she chased the boys to bed and went back into the bathroom.

Holiday sat up and looked around her. She had been lucky enough to land in the lap of a big teddy bear. Jodi was half in and half out of the box that held Holiday's former wardrobe, as stiff and glassy-eyed as ever.

I guess she really is just a doll. Holiday sighed.

She had started to settle down on the teddy bear's lap when a movement caught her eye. Zorro was watching her hungrily from his lair under Jennifer's bed.

## Conversation on a Bear

"Don't give me any trouble," Holiday warned him.

But it looked as if trouble was just what Zorro had in mind. He began to slink forward, his eyes boring into Holiday's. She jumped off the bear's lap and looked around for something to defend herself with.

"I'm warning you, cat," she said.

"Pull his whiskers," a voice from behind her advised. "That's something he can't stand."

Holiday turned and stared. Jodi was on her feet beside the box of clothes, brushing herself off and patting at her hair.

"You *are* alive," Holiday breathed.

"Look out!" Jodi said sharply.

A soft paw knocked Holiday flat on the floor, and curved claws held her there. She looked up into the glittering eyes of Zorro. He loosened his claws and gave Holiday a little push. When she got up to run, he slapped her down again.

With a yell, Jodi ran to the cat and grabbed one of his whiskers in both hands. She leaned back, pulling on it with all her weight. The cat yowled, shook himself free, and retreated to the safety of his hideout under the bed. He crouched there, rubbing his cheek with his paw and scowling at the dolls.

"And stay there, or I'll do it again," Jodi said threateningly.

Holiday didn't even glance at the cat. Her interest was all in Jodi.

"I knew you were alive!" she said. "I told Caitlin but she said you weren't."

"Is it true that she really misses me?" Jodi asked.

Just then Jennifer came into the room, and Holiday and Jodi had to go back to being normal dolls. Without a glance in their direction Jennifer changed into her nightgown and got into bed.

Caitlin would have said good-night to us, Holiday thought.

The two dolls stayed quiet and still until they could tell by Jennifer's breathing that she was asleep. Then Jodi scrambled to her feet and grabbed Holiday by the arm.

"Is it true?" she asked again. "Does Caitlin really want me back?"

Holiday pulled her arm away.

"Yes, it's true," she said, bracing herself for a happy outburst from Jodi.

But Jodi didn't look as overjoyed as Holiday had expected her to be.

"Aren't you glad?" she asked.

# Conversation on a Bear

"Well, sure," Jodi said. "But I wish I'd known before. I wouldn't have done all those things to get her in trouble with her friends."

Holiday stared. "You were trying to get *Caitlin* in trouble?"

"Well, what would *you* do if *you* were dumped in a box and left all alone for no reason?" Jodi asked resentfully. "How would *you* feel?"

Holiday was angry with Caitlin, too, but she couldn't help defending her. "Jodi, she didn't think you'd care. She thought you were just a doll."

"Just a doll!" Jodi said, flaring up. "What kind of excuse is that? Dolls have feelings, too, don't they?"

"Not usually," Holiday said.

At her words Jodi stood still and stared at Holiday.

"You're right," she said slowly. "In fact, at the time I'm not sure that I—"

Holiday was too full of her own thoughts to listen. "Anyway, *I'm* the one you got into trouble," she said. "Caitlin thinks I'm stealing my clothes back."

Jodi put her hand over her mouth. "Oops," she said.

"And I want you to tell her that she's wrong," Holiday said.

Jodi gasped. "I can't do that."

# DOLL TROUBLE

"You have to," Holiday insisted. "You have to tell her about the ski jacket and the jeans and about crawling into her bag."

"I was running away." Jodi's chin began to quiver. "I don't want to move away with Jennifer."

"You don't have to move away," Holiday said. "I'm personally going to get you back with Caitlin. But you have to promise to tell her she was wrong about me."

"But then she won't take me back," Jodi whimpered. "She already gave me away once, and I hadn't even done anything then."

"Fine, don't tell her." Holiday shrugged. "You can just live here forever with Jennifer and her brothers and that cat."

Jodi shuddered. "I'll tell her," she said.

"Okay." Holiday became businesslike. "Now let's figure out how to get you away from Jennifer."

They sat facing each other, one on each of the teddy bear's furry legs, and discussed the situation.

"Does Jennifer know you can talk?" Holiday asked.

"Certainly not," Jodi said coldly. "I have nothing to say to Jennifer. Nothing nice, anyway."

"Good," Holiday said. "That will make it easier. Now,

# Conversation on a Bear

the first thing we need to do is to let Caitlin know that you're alive."

"You could do that when she comes to get you tomorrow," Jodi suggested.

"I *did* tell her," Holiday said with an angry flush. "She didn't believe me."

"Oh. I'll tell her then," Jodi said. "No, I'll show her. I'll wink or wiggle my ears or something."

Holiday looked at Jodi with interest. "Can you really wiggle your ears?"

Jodi showed her that she could, and then Holiday tried it, too. She wiggled her nose and her eyes and her lips, but her ears never even twitched. The dolls nearly fell off the bear, laughing.

When they settled down again, Jodi said, "But what good will it do when Caitlin knows I'm alive? She can't just ask for me back. Jennifer wouldn't give me to her."

"No, you're right," Holiday agreed. She sat in silent concentration for a few minutes, and then she said, "Would she sell you, do you think?"

"She probably would," Jodi said resentfully. "She's been trying to get enough money together to buy a TV for her room."

"A TV!" Holiday exclaimed. "I hope she wouldn't ask for *that* much money."

"I'm certainly worth as much as a TV," Jodi said huffily.

Holiday didn't hear her. She was thinking about the money.

"I know Caitlin has some saved," she said.

She didn't mention that the money was being put aside for something special for Holiday. Caitlin and Holiday had seen it at the mall—a red car with a white top that really went up and down and a super sound system. Caitlin loved it as much as Holiday did, even though she would never be able to ride in it.

But now Holiday was going away. There wouldn't be any red convertible. Caitlin could use all the money to buy Jodi back. It was very hard for Holiday to give up the chance to own that car. She was sure that Jodi would never be able to do such an unselfish thing.

I'm so brave, she thought. Caitlin is losing a wonderful doll.

But she couldn't think about that now. There were plans to make.

"What we'll do," she decided, "is just wait here quietly until tomorrow. Caitlin is sure to come over first thing to see if Jennifer has found me yet."

"When she walks in the door, I'll wiggle my ears at her," Jodi said. "Won't she be surprised?"

Both dolls broke into laughter at the thought of Caitlin's expression. Then from across the room came another laugh, high-pitched and excited. Holiday and Jodi froze, staring at each other in horror.

"Jennifer's awake," Holiday groaned. "We woke her up."

# CHAPTER 15

## Jennifer's Scare

Holiday and Jodi slowly turned toward the bed. Jennifer was gazing at them in fascination.

"She knows we're alive," Jodi murmured. "She'll never let us go now."

# Jennifer's Scare

"Hello, dolls," Jennifer called softly. She laughed again. "This dream seems so real."

Holiday and Jodi looked at each other.

"Can she really think she's dreaming?" Jodi asked.

Holiday broke into a gleeful giggle.

"Watch this," she told Jodi.

She jumped off the teddy bear's leg and searched quickly through the box of doll clothes. She pulled out a large lacy stole and flung it around her shoulders.

"Holiday," Jodi whispered anxiously, "what are you doing?"

"I have a plan," Holiday whispered back.

She walked regally to Jennifer's bedside.

"You are right," she said. "This dream seems very real, but it is definitely a dream." She glanced back at Jodi and giggled and then turned again to Jennifer. "You will be honored to know," she continued, "that I, the queen of the doll world, am visiting you in your dream."

"Holiday," Jodi whispered more anxiously, "what are you saying?"

Jennifer sat up straighter, looking interested.

"You just look like Caitlin's Holiday to me," she said.

"Yes, I was visiting the world of humans for a time," Holiday said grandly. "Now I must get back to my kingdom, and I am taking Jodi with me. I now command you to go down and open the door for us."

"This is an amazing dream," Jennifer said. "I hope Matt and Skip will be in it."

"Forget Matt and Skip," Holiday said. "Just get up and take Jodi and me downstairs and put us outside. My subjects are waiting to take us back to my kingdom."

"Jodi?" Jennifer asked. "Do you mean Caitlin's old Jodi? What would she be doing here?"

"I mean Wendi," Holiday said hastily. She had forgotten that Jennifer had renamed Jodi. "In my kingdom she is known as Jodi."

Holiday was enjoying herself. It was fun playing queen. She threw an end of the stole over her shoulder dramatically.

"Get up now and open the door for us," she commanded, "and we will be on our way."

"No," Jennifer said. "I don't want you to go."

Holiday was surprised. She had expected Jennifer to hop right up and let them out. In fact, Holiday had almost begun to believe that she really *was* queen of the doll world.

"I must insist that we leave immediately," she said.

"It's my dream," Jennifer said, "so we have to do what I want."

"It's not working," Jodi said in an urgent undertone. "Let her go back to sleep."

"Shh," Holiday said, and she turned royally back to Jennifer.

"As a matter of fact," she said, "this is not a dream. This is real life. I am a real queen, and I command you to open the door and let us out."

Jennifer just laughed.

"If this isn't a dream, I own two real live dolls," she said. "Do you think I would let go of real live dolls? Real live dolls are extremely rare, even in dreams."

"You're making it worse," Jodi muttered.

But Holiday wasn't ready to give up. She pulled the stole over her head, held it under her chin with one hand, and extended her other arm, pointing threateningly toward Jennifer.

"If you do not let us go," she intoned, "you will suffer serious consequences."

# DOLL TROUBLE

Jodi covered her face with her hands. "Oh, no," she groaned.

"Like what?" Jennifer asked. She didn't sound afraid, just curious.

Holiday hadn't thought that far yet.

"Well, let's see," she considered. "I know." She pointed toward Jennifer again. "Every night while you sleep, I will climb up on your bed and cut off a piece of your hair."

Jodi rolled her eyes toward the ceiling. "Oh, Holiday, that's so dumb," she whispered.

"Then," Holiday continued, "when you are all bald, I will draw a different picture on your head every night with magic ink that you can't wash off, and this will go on forever and you will hate it."

"No, I won't. It sounds pretty. Oh, look," Jennifer said, looking pleased. "Zorro's in my dream."

"Uh-oh," Holiday said.

She had been too busy playing her role to remember that the cat was in the audience. Now he had decided to take a part in the show. He edged toward Holiday and reached out a tentative paw.

Holiday stamped her foot. "Get," she said.

# Jennifer's Scare

The cat hesitated, flattening his ears and glaring at her.

"I said, 'get,'" Holiday said more forcefully.

The cat thought it over, his eyes moving back and forth from Holiday to Jodi. Then he turned and leaped up onto the bed. He walked across Jennifer and settled down beside her, still glaring at the dolls.

Jennifer touched the cat's fur with her fingertips and quickly pulled her hand back as if she had touched something hot. "Wait a minute," she said, her eyes opening wide. "I'm awake."

"I told you that already," Holiday said, but Jennifer wasn't listening.

"I'm not dreaming," she went on, looking more terrified every minute. "Zorro feels too real. And this is too weird. I would never dream anything this weird."

"I told you you were overdoing it," Jodi whispered.

Holiday was afraid Jodi was right. She hadn't expected Jennifer to get so scared. But she hadn't given up yet. She just had to keep Jennifer calm long enough to get them out of there.

"Now," Holiday urged, trying to speak soothingly and quickly at the same time, "if you'll just take us downstairs and open the door for us, we won't bother you anymore."

But Jennifer had lost control.

"Mommy! Daddy!" she shrieked. "Come quick!"

Holiday and Jodi dropped to the floor as Jennifer's father, mother, and two excited brothers came crowding into the room.

"Did you see a monster?" Matt asked hopefully.

"The dolls are alive!" Jennifer screamed.

Nobody even glanced at the dolls. All their concern was for Jennifer.

"They were talking and walking around!" she yelled.

"You had a nightmare," Jennifer's father told her.

"They wanted me to let them outside!" Jennifer screeched.

Jennifer's mother sat down beside her on the bed.

"It's all right," she said reassuringly. "The cat woke you up and scared you. Your father forgot to let it out."

"*I* forgot?" Jennifer's father asked. "Am I the only person in this family capable of putting out the cat? Am I the only one who can turn a doorknob?"

"It wasn't the cat. It was the dolls," Jennifer insisted loudly.

# Jennifer's Scare

"I've got to get some sleep," Jennifer's father said. "Come on, you."

He lunged at Zorro, but the cat twisted away and leaped to the floor. Holiday was lying in his path, and as he bounded across her, his hind claws caught in the threads of her stole.

He'll ruin it, Holiday thought in annoyance.

She hung on, trying to pull it loose. Instead she found herself being swooped through the air. Jennifer's father had grabbed Zorro, and the stole had come, too. Muttering not-very-nice things about the cat, he thudded down the stairs, unlocked the front door, and heaved Zorro outside. The stole went with the cat, and so did Holiday.

# CHAPTER 16

## Riding Zorro

The front door slammed, and Holiday and the cat were alone on the sidewalk. They sat still for a moment, both a little dazed by their sudden exit from the house. Then Zorro began trying to shake the stole from his hind paws.

## Riding Zorro

"Wait, I'll do it," Holiday said. "You'll pull the threads."

The cat looked thoughtfully at Holiday, and she began to regret attracting his attention.

"Never mind. Keep the stole," she said. "I have to get going."

She tried to walk casually past him, but Zorro stopped her with a velvety paw. He pushed her gently, and she staggered.

"Stop it," she said angrily. "I'm in a hurry."

Her anger didn't faze the cat. He pushed her again.

"Zorro, I mean it," she said sternly. "Leave me alone."

But Zorro was delighted with his new toy. He batted Holiday from one paw to the other until she was dizzy.

"I am not enjoying this, Zorro," she told him.

Actually she thought it might be fun to play with the cat, but this was not a convenient time. She wanted to get home to Caitlin. It would be a long walk for doll-size legs, and she was anxious to get started.

How can I get rid of this cat? she wondered, and then she remembered Zorro's sensitive whiskers. All she had to do was grab them the way Jodi had done. She made several tries, but the cat kept her so off balance that she missed every time. Holiday was becoming very irritated.

"I'm a doll, Zorro," she complained, "not a catnip mouse."

That gave her an idea. She had seen cats lose interest in live mice when the mice stopped trying to escape. Maybe it would work with her. She let herself drop in a limp heap on the sidewalk. When Zorro slapped at her, she flopped about as loosely as a rag doll. The cat looked confused and disappointed. He thrust his face close to Holiday and sniffed. In a sudden move she reached out and clutched one of his whiskers.

The cat yowled and shook his head, and Holiday was jerked violently back and forth through the air. She gripped the whisker tightly, but it was slippery, and she felt it sliding through her hands. Then Zorro threw his head down and up in a way that broke Holiday's hold completely. She flipped up in the air and felt herself land on something that was not pavement and not grass. It was rough and hairy and wobbly. The cat had tossed her onto his own back.

Holiday grabbed handfuls of fur to keep herself from sliding down to the ground again. Once she had her balance, she pulled herself onto the nape of Zorro's neck, wrapping both legs and both arms as far around him as she could.

Zorro went wild, and Holiday shrieked with excitement. The cat jumped and shook himself. He even rolled on the ground, but through everything Holiday clung to him like chewing gum. It was the most thrilling ride she had ever had, much better than Caitlin's bike.

I wish Caitlin could see me, she thought. She'd be so impressed.

But while riding the cat was fun, it wasn't getting Holiday home. She wondered what she should do next.

If I get off, she thought, he'll just start pestering me again.

Zorro's antics had worked the stole off his claw. Now he had stopped rolling and was simply running around and around in a tight circle.

I'll just have to hang on until he's too tired to chase me, Holiday thought, but she didn't want to do that. It might take a long time, and besides, she was getting dizzy.

"Zorro, stop!" she commanded, and she took hold of his ears and pulled.

Zorro didn't seem to notice. He continued to run in a circle, and Holiday felt more dizzy all the time.

I'll fall off in a minute, she thought. Then I'll be back where I started.

Then Holiday had an idea. The cat was running to the left, so Holiday reached out with her right hand, grabbed a bunch of whiskers, and pulled. Zorro threw his head back, and then to Holiday's delight, he changed direction. Now, instead of running to the left, he began running in circles to the right.

With rising excitement Holiday let go of the whiskers and then, changing hands, she pulled the whiskers on the left side of Zorro's head. The cat swung to the left. She did it again, just to make sure it hadn't been accidental. When she pulled Zorro's right whiskers, he turned to the right. When she pulled his left-side whiskers, he turned to the left.

"I can steer a cat!" Holiday yelled triumphantly.

She waved her arms in the air so vigorously that she nearly lost her balance. The close call calmed her down. Squeezing her knees tightly against the cat's neck, she leaned forward and held the cat's whiskers in both hands as if they were reins.

"Zorro," she said, "you're going to take me home to Caitlin."

# CHAPTER 17

# Behind the Flower Pot

Riding Zorro was a much speedier way to Caitlin's than walking. The cat seemed to feel that if he ran fast enough, he would be able to run out from under Holiday. It made for a wild ride, but Holiday held on tightly,

**111**

pulling the cat's whiskers right or left as necessary to keep him headed in the right direction.

Zorro streaked along the sidewalk, ignoring traffic and red lights, and before Holiday had thought of a way to slow him down, they were at Caitlin's. There was nothing to do then but let go and roll off.

It was a rough landing. Holiday bounced and bumped for several feet before she smacked up against the brick wall of the sub shop across the street from Caitlin's house. She sat leaning against the wall, watching the cat disappear up the street.

Poor Zorro, she thought. I hope he doesn't get lost.

From where she sat she could see Caitlin's bedroom window. The room was dark.

It would be nice if Caitlin was sitting there, watching for me, Holiday thought. But of course, she wasn't.

Suddenly Holiday felt very tired and very alone. The catback ride had been fun, but nothing else she had tried to do tonight had worked. She had done everything wrong. Now Jennifer knew that Jodi was alive. She would never let Caitlin have her back. Jodi would have to move away with Jennifer. Caitlin would always miss her.

# Behind the Flower Pot

And even worse, Holiday thought, Caitlin will always think I was taking the clothes.

It began to drizzle, but Holiday was so depressed that she didn't give a thought to her hair or her clothes. They were a wreck, anyway, after the night's activities. Still, she thought she'd better get out of sight. The cat might come back, and she didn't feel like dealing with him again so soon.

When she was sure there was no one watching, she ran across the street as quickly as she could and crawled behind a pot of geraniums that Caitlin's mother had put on the step. The spot wasn't protected from the rain, which was nicer for the geraniums than it was for Holiday, but she didn't have the energy to look for a better hiding place. So all night long she sat there, getting wetter and wetter, feeling sorry for Jodi, sorry for Caitlin, and very, very sorry for herself.

Around dawn it stopped raining. The geraniums had had more than enough water, and the excess had overflowed onto Holiday, but she wasn't thinking about that. She was counting the hours until Caitlin would come outside and find her. They had been apart for only one night, but to Holiday it seemed like months.

# DOLL TROUBLE

At last the porch door swung open. Holiday quickly leaped to her feet and then just as quickly crouched again. It was Caitlin's father on his way to work. Holiday had forgotten about him because she usually wasn't up when he left in the morning. He got into his truck, which was parked at the curb, and left without a glance toward the muddy face half hidden by geranium blossoms.

The sun rose higher and the traffic thickened and Holiday grew more and more impatient. Where was Caitlin? She often ate her breakfast sitting on the steps with Holiday beside her. Holiday's throat tightened. Would they ever have nice times like that again?

The porch door opened again, slowly this time, and Holiday held her breath. It was Caitlin at last. She came outside and sat on the step, staring listlessly toward the street.

Holiday stayed behind the pot. She had waited anxiously for Caitlin the whole long night, but now that she was so close, Holiday was afraid. Would Caitlin be mad at her? Maybe she thought that Holiday was the one who had hidden Jodi yesterday. What if she said, "Go away"? What if she said, "I hate you"?

What's wrong with me? Holiday wondered disgustedly. Why don't I just walk right up to Caitlin and say, "Good morning?" Or I could say, "Why do you like Jodi better than me?" Or I could say, "Because of your lack of trust in me—"

In the middle of Holiday's plans, Caitlin stood up. She was going back inside.

"Wait!" Holiday screamed.

Caitlin's eyes popped as she watched her doll struggle out from behind the flower pot.

"Holiday!" she exclaimed. She grabbed the doll and kissed her dirty face. "Oh, Holiday, I've been so worried."

Holiday burst into tears. "I've been worried, too."

Caitlin kissed her again and again.

"Don't cry," she said. "You're home now. That's all that matters."

Then Holiday knew that she would never play the dramatic good-bye scene she had imagined. It would have been fun, but it wasn't going to happen because Holiday wasn't going away. No matter what Caitlin believed about her, no matter what Jodi did, no matter what Jennifer said, Holiday was going to stay with Caitlin forever.

# CHAPTER 18

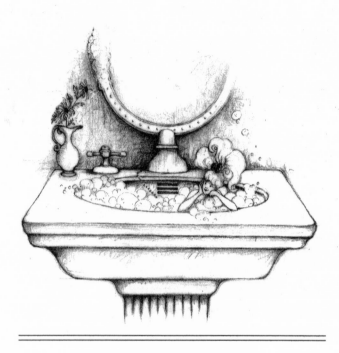

# A Surprise Gift

Caitlin took Holiday upstairs, filled the washbasin with
warm water, and gave it a big squirt of bubble bath.
She undressed Holiday and let her soak among the
bubbles until she was calm again. Then she washed

**116**

## A Surprise Gift

Holiday's mud- and tear-streaked face and her gold-silver hair, wrapped her in a soft towel, and carried her into the bedroom. She laid her gently in the little doll bed and sat on the floor beside her.

"You wouldn't be so nice if you knew how I've messed everything up," Holiday said in a shaky voice.

"Nothing's messed up," Caitlin said. "Now that you're back, everything is fine."

Holiday shook her head.

"I wanted Jodi to tell you about the clothes," she said unhappily.

"Guess what," Caitlin said. "I've got a job now. I'll be able to buy you lots of nice clothes. Then maybe you'll stop thinking so much about the ones I made you lose."

"I don't think about—" Holiday began, and then she realized what Caitlin had said. "A job?"

"Well, sort of," Caitlin said. "Mrs. Rigby says she'll give me a dollar every time I straighten up the shop."

"I saw you come out of there yesterday," Holiday remembered. "I thought you didn't want to do things with me anymore."

"Oh, Holiday, how could you think that?" Caitlin asked.

"I can't help it," Holiday said. "I know how you're always thinking about Jodi."

"I am not," Caitlin said. "But what about you, always wishing for your clothes back?"

"I am not," Holiday said. "I don't care about those clothes."

"Then, Holiday," Caitlin asked, "why do you keep taking them?"

Holiday jumped out of bed and began fishing underwear out of her box of clothes. She dressed rapidly, grumbling the whole time. "After all I've been through." She jerked on her jeans. "Trapped in a medicine cabinet. Riding a cat." She popped her head through the neck of her T-shirt and glared at Caitlin. "And to you I'm just a crook."

"Wait a minute," Caitlin said. "Did you just say you rode a cat in a medicine cabinet?"

"No, I didn't say that," Holiday said.

"It sounded like it to me," Caitlin said.

"Then you're not a good listener," Holiday told her. "But the thing is, Caitlin, I was trying to bring Jodi home to you, but now that Jennifer knows that Jodi's alive, she'll never let her go, no matter how much of my car money you offer her."

# A Surprise Gift

Caitlin put her hand on Holiday's forehead. "Do dolls get feverish?" she asked. "I think you're delirious."

Holiday pushed her hand away crossly. "I'm not feverish, and I'm not delirious, either, whatever that is. It's just that you never believe anything I say."

"Well, then," Caitlin said, "say something I can believe."

In her mind Holiday ran over the things she wanted to tell Caitlin. She thought of the hours in the medicine cabinet and of Jodi speaking at last and the fun of pretending to be in Jennifer's dream. She thought about her wild ride home in the dark on Zorro's back. Was all that something that Caitlin could believe? Probably not, but at least she was ready to listen.

"Sit down," Holiday said. "This is a long story."

Caitlin made herself comfortable on the floor beside Holiday.

"Wait until you see what a good listener I can be," she said.

But Holiday had barely begun to speak when the doorbell rang. Caitlin made an impatient sound and ran downstairs to answer it. Holiday sat on the side of her bed and waited. She heard the door open, heard a murmur of voices, heard the door shut again. She heard

# DOLL TROUBLE

Caitlin gallop up the stairs and heard the surprise and joy in her voice as she said, "Look what Jennifer just gave me!"

Holiday looked. Caitlin was holding her old doll Jodi.

# CHAPTER 19

# Magic

Holiday could hardly believe her eyes. "Why would Jennifer give you Jodi?"

"Because she's scared of me," Jodi said.

Caitlin screamed in surprise and dropped the doll on the floor. She stared, speechless, as Jodi jumped to her feet and stood there, giggling up at her. Holiday danced around them excitedly.

"I told you she was alive," she said gleefully. To Jodi she said, "Is Jennifer really scared of you?"

Jodi nodded, her eyes glinting with mischief. "It's because of you," she said. "Those crazy things you told her last night."

Both dolls laughed delightedly.

"On the way here," Jodi added, "Jennifer said, 'I just wish I could see Caitlin's face when the queen of the doll world comes after you.'"

The two dolls roared. Caitlin watched them with a dazed expression.

"Will somebody tell me what's been going on?" she asked.

So Holiday finally got to tell her story. Jodi had a lot to say, too. Often both were talking at once, and they even acted out scenes with one or the other taking the part of Jennifer or Zorro or even Jennifer's father. Before the story was finished, Caitlin and her dolls were weak with laughter.

Finally Caitlin said, "There's one thing I don't understand." She looked at Jodi curiously. "When you were my doll, why didn't you ever talk to me?"

# Magic

"Didn't I?" Jodi asked. "I can't remember." She frowned in thought. "No matter how hard I try, I can't recall anything before the day we went swimming in Lauren's pool."

"The day Jennifer stuck her big foot in the water and ducked us," Holiday said resentfully.

"I just remember lying by the pool," Jennifer said. "I was sad. And I was wearing something that itched."

"My old cloak," Holiday said. "It's scratchy because it has metallic threads."

She felt annoyed all over again thinking of how Jennifer used her beautiful cloak as a beach robe. Then another thought struck her, and she forgot all about Jennifer.

"That old cloak!" she said excitedly. "I just realized. I never knew before! But it must be! I'm sure of it!"

Caitlin and Jodi stared at Holiday.

"It's magic," Holiday exclaimed, but Caitlin and Jodi continued to stare.

"It's magic," Holiday repeated. "Jodi was never alive until Jennifer put that cloak on her."

"That doesn't prove anything," Caitlin said. "How could a cloak do that, anyway?"

"How do I know?" Holiday asked. "But it did. I can

**123**

remember a lot farther back than Jodi can. But in my very first memory I'm wearing that same cloak!"

They all sat staring at each other.

"Do you think?" Caitlin asked.

"Do you suppose?" Jodi asked.

"I *know!*" said Holiday. "Now, let's plan how we can get my cloak away from Jennifer. Who knows what she'll wrap in it next?"

"Jennifer doesn't have it anymore," Jodi said.

Holiday's face fell. "Did she throw it away?"

Jodi shook her head. "On the way here she stopped at Lauren's and gave her all the clothes. She didn't want us to have them."

All at the same time the three of them realized what that meant. Big grins spread across their faces.

"Lauren has the cloak," Jodi said.

"She'll try it on Sandi," Holiday continued.

"Sandi will become a live doll like you two," Caitlin concluded.

Holiday jumped up and did perfect cartwheels all the way across the room.

"We're going to have so much fun together," she said. "I'll teach you and Sandi all my games."

# Magic

She ran to the window and climbed up the curtain to the windowsill. "This one is called Surprise the Driver."

"But you're not allowed to play it," Caitlin said.

"But we're not allowed to play it," Holiday said.

She sat down on the sill and looked out the window. "Here comes Lauren," she said. "She's carrying Sandi. She's in a hurry. And she's talking with stiff lips."

Caitlin ran to the window. "Hi, Lauren," she called. "What's the matter with your lips?"

"Caitlin!" Lauren yelled excitedly. "Come quick! I have something amazing to tell you!"

"I know you do." Caitlin laughed.

She scooped up her two live dolls and ran downstairs. For once Holiday didn't turn back into a normal, stiff doll as Caitlin rushed down the steps. She tried, but she found it impossible to keep from smiling.

It was fun when it was just Caitlin and me, she thought, but this will be even better.

She laughed, thinking of all the fun they would have together.

I got Jodi back with Caitlin, she thought with satisfaction, and I still have all of my car money.

# DOLL TROUBLE

Lauren, wild with excitement, was waiting for them at the front door.

"Look!" she said, holding out her doll, and Sandi, wrapped in the mysterious old cloak, smiled a shy, friendly smile.